For our friends in Lecchi in Chianti

In the first book about Cinta (*cheen*-ta), the naughty pig's
adventures took him—magically—all through a huge
painting in the town hall of Siena in Italy.
This photo shows only the part of the picture
where the artist painted the pig walking with his master.

The artist, named Ambrogio Lorenzetti,
created the painting about 670 years ago.
It is called *The Effects of Good Government in the City
and Countryside.* You can see the whole painting
—and Cinta—in the town hall on Siena's main square.

Now, in this second book, the pig Cinta escapes to the city
of Florence and magically enters a painting there,
The Journey of the Magi, the Three Kings.
It was painted by Benozzo Gozzoli in the Chapel
of the Medici (*meh*-dee-chee) family's palace
about 550 years ago. This photo shows the youngest king
in a tiny part of the large painting.

Of course, Cinta does not know the story of the Magi
who traveled from the East, bringing fabulous gifts
to the Christ Child, but Cinta loves the procession
and its amazing characters. You will see.

Mandragora s.r.l.
Piazza del Duomo 9, 50122 Firenze
www.mandragora.it

Edited, designed and typeset by
Monica Fintoni, Andrea Paoletti, Paola Vannucchi

Photographs
Studio Lensini, Siena
Antonio Quattrone, Florence

Printed in Italy by Alpilito, Florence

ISBN 978-88-7461-158-4

Nancy Shroyer Howard

More Mischief in Tuscany

ADVENTURES IN A FLORENTINE MASTERPIECE

Mandragora

Here is another story about me, Cinta (*cheen*-ta).
I am the best kind of pig, a Cinta Senese pig—Cinta
from the Italian word for belt and Senese for Siena.
I live in a famous painting in Siena.

For over 670 years I have lived in the same old painting.
I love my painting—and my pigpen—but now
I want some excitement…
in another famous painting, in another adventure!

Is it possible?

In his pigpen, the day began quite badly for Cinta.
His master trudged off to the market in Siena
leaving Cinta behind.
Instead of Cinta, his master took two skinny chickens.
Worse, his master forgot Cinta's breakfast.
His stone trough was empty. So was his stomach.
A growling came out from under his handsome white belt.

Cinta had never tried to escape.
He was well fed and, besides, he was a bit timid.
Now Cinta longed for adventure.
"I will just run away!" he exclaimed bravely.
"If my master has gone off without me in one direction,
I will run away in the opposite direction."
The gate was closed.
Cinta noticed for the first time
that the wall was low.
"I will just leap over it,"
he decided.

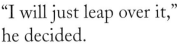

It wasn't easy.

Cinta picked himself up and ran as fast
as a pig could run, which is very fast.
"Perhaps I am being followed," he thought.
After a long while, he stopped
and glanced back. No one.

He looked around.
"This is a strange new place.
Everything is tall here:
the trees, the pointed hills,
the towers of the white castle
that is about to fall off a mountaintop."

"I will run up the road to that castle,"
he decided. "Then I will slide down again
on a bumpy slope and see where I land."

"Wheeeeeeeee! I think
I am beginning to have an adventure!"

Cinta landed headfirst in the top of a prickly tree.
"Oweeee!"

He wriggled himself down and shook himself off.
"Perhaps I will find some breakfast. Yes! There is
a vineyard. I love grapes!" He raced toward the vineyard.

Running in and out of the rows of grapevines,
Cinta searched for purple or yellow bunches of grapes.

"Oh," he groaned, "they have all been harvested."

Cinta struggled up a hillside and collapsed onto the rocks.

Cinta woke to the sound of a dog barking.
A shepherd rested on his staff and paid no attention.
The dog snarled at Cinta, "Stay away from our sheep."
Cinta leapt past him, frightened.
"Where are you going?" howled the dog.
"Away!" snorted Cinta, and he raced off.

Cinta raced right into a donkey, whose startled ears
stood straight out. "Have you anything to eat?"
begged Cinta. "I am hungry myself," replied the ass,
"but you may drink from this pond."

Cinta gulped some water.
"May I eat the reeds? They look fat and juicy."
The donkey nodded, doubtfully.
Off the brown top of a reed, Cinta took a huge bite.
Fuzzy seeds exploded in his mouth and sailed into the air.
The donkey sneezed and so did Cinta.
"Kachooooooo!" "Kachooooooo!"

"Acorns suit a pig much better,"
muttered Cinta.

MY DONKEY
SNEEZES?

On the other side
of the hill, Cinta found
another flock of sheep.
Their shepherd was tired.
One of the sheep explained,
"All through the night
we have walked down
from the hills. Our shepherd
was following a star."
"Leading you where?"
asked Cinta.
"We do not know,"
replied the sheep.

"I know where *I* am going,"
Cinta announced.
"To see everything there
is beyond my pigpen!"
The sheep thought
a moment.
"That may take a few days."
"Oh?" said Cinta.

He wandered on slowly and stumbled right into an ox.
Cinta looked up at the ox. "I am so tired," he sniffled.
"I would carry you," the ox replied,
"but my master is saving me for important work."
"I hope to have important *adventures*," bragged Cinta.
"Then," advised the ox, "you had better rest first."

Cinta lay down under the soft nose of the ox.

When Cinta awoke, the ox was gone,
but an amazing procession appeared before him.

"A parade!" he squeeled. "Lots of people! Lots of mules!
And look at those two lumpy creatures with long necks
and knobby knees! I think I will ride them."

Cinta grabbed their two tails, leapt high in the air,
and landed in just the right place. "Yippeeeeeee!"
The creatures jumped, shuddered, shivered,
and shook their humps. Cinta was dumped into the dust.
"What a fine ride!" he announced. He felt triumphant.

But no one noticed, not even the girl in the red dress.

DID I HEAR SOMETHING?

JUST A LITTLE THUMP
IN THE ROAD.

Just then, Cinta saw another amazing procession.
"More mules! Two more lumpy creatures! Beautiful boxes!
Are they full of fruits and acorns?"

Cinta squealed with delight, "Eeeeeeeeeeeeeeee!"
This terrified the animals.
The lumpy creatures kicked up their heels.
The mules reared up onto their back legs.
Bundles and boxes went flying and broke open.

Treasures spilled out and glistened in the sunlight.
Cinta bent to gobble a few. They were hard
and not at all sweet. He snorted and spit them out.

It was then that he spotted another astounding scene.

A small cat rode by on a powerful brown horse.
A larger cat strained to stare at Cinta.
Both cats had spots—even down their tails.

Curious, Cinta asked,
"Do you have spots because you are ill?"
"No, you silly pig," snarled the large cat, insulted.
"We are *supposed* to have spots. We are cheetahs,
pets of princes. We hunt with kings."
"I hunt, too," said Cinta proudly. "I hunt for acorns!"
The big cat sneered. "Well, *we* ride on horseback."
"Well," bragged Cinta, "*I* ride on animals with lumps
on their backs!" He did not say that he was dumped.

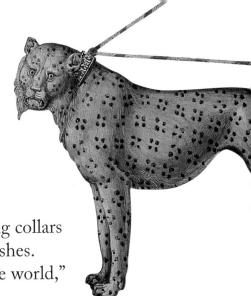

The cats showed off their glowing collars
and they rattled their jeweled leashes.
"We are the fastest animals in the world,"
claimed the yellow cheetah.
"Oh no," responded Cinta. "I can run
much faster because…"
"Absurd," interrupted the furious grey cheetah.
"Impossible," added the yellow one.
Cinta continued, "… because I wear no collar
and I am not on a leash."

Cinta danced off freely.
He could not resist.

Cinta danced right into a magnificent sight.
Shining objects shimmered in the hand of one rider,
on the head of an old man, and even on the harness
of a white mule. Cinta was astonished.

A duck whispered, "That is the great King Melchior
from the East. The decorations are made of gold.
Important people love gold."
"I love it, too," said Cinta importantly,
"but it tastes terrible."
"Well then," said the duck. "Nibble some green plants.
And then have a swim."
"Oh yes!" exclaimed Cinta. "I am so dusty and itchy.
May I roll and wallow?
Will there be mud?"

Just as Cinta shook himself dry,
another king appeared, more splendid than the first.
"Make way for King Balthazar!" called a page.
Cinta and the duck jumped aside.
Balthazar's horse, with its golden harness, was stupendous.
Balthazar himself was stupendous in his sparkling gown,
his jeweled and feathered crown.

Cinta longed to look splendid.
He wished for a fine hat.

Cinta imagined himself in a hat
—and in red and blue legs, riding
like a cheetah behind the King.

The sound of tramping hooves brought
Cinta to his senses.

Another parade appeared!
A long-eared brown donkey
explained, "We are on a journey
to Bethlehem with the famous
Cosimo de' Medici.
He rides on me—that is why
I wear golden harness!"
Cinta envied not the gold
but the rider's red hat!

Then a blaze of light
caught Cinta's eye.

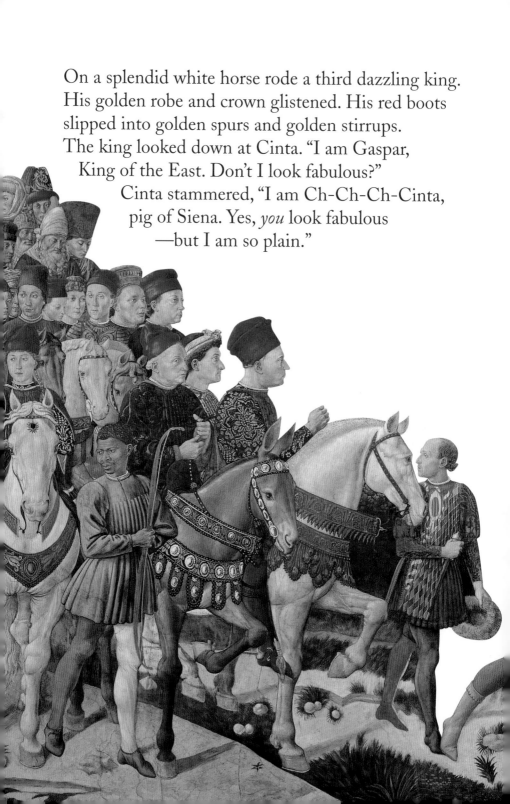

On a splendid white horse rode a third dazzling king.
His golden robe and crown glistened. His red boots
slipped into golden spurs and golden stirrups.
The king looked down at Cinta. "I am Gaspar,
King of the East. Don't I look fabulous?"
Cinta stammered, "I am Ch-Ch-Ch-Cinta,
pig of Siena. Yes, *you* look fabulous
—but I am so plain."

Cinta sprang onto the rocks,
snatched a red hat
and jumped away.

DID ANYONE SEE MY RED HAT?

Cinta landed flat on his back.

Kaboom!

When he could breathe again, Cinta looked up.

Three men, kings' pages—with weapons—stood over him.
The page with the spear said, "This pig thinks he can steal
our guest's hat! How shall we punish him?"

The page with the bow and arrow said,
"Let's have roast pig for dinner!"

"Good idea," said the third page.

Cinta had never heard such a bad idea. He was terrified.

"This will be the end of me," he wailed.
A page began to poke with his spear around Cinta's
belly and ribs. This tickled Cinta and made him giggle.
"Eeee. Hee hee!" Then he broadcast an enormous,
roaring laughter. "Eeeeeeeee. Whoooaaa. Yeeeee. Yow!"

Cinta's horrendous roar horrified the three pages.
They ran off holding their ears.
"What an exciting drama!" grunted Cinta happily.
He forgot about the hat.

Looking up and above King Gaspar,
Cinta spied a new drama. A hunter was chasing
a beautiful deer. Cinta gave his very loudest snort.
"Snnnnnnnnnort!"
This spooked the hunter, who was chasing the deer.
This spooked the hunter's galloping horse.
This spooked the hunter's hound.

The hunter lost his balance. He lost his spear.
The hound did a somersault.
The deer skipped to safety.

Cinta, looking further up the hill, spied another drama.

"Help!"

A hare was hiding in tall grass.
A hound was sniffing for it.
"I do not like big dogs sniffing
for harmless creatures," growled Cinta.
"To the rescue!"

Cinta climbed up and over the sharp rocks
as fast as a pig could climb.
He lowered his head.
The bristles on his back stood straight up.
He felt that he had the tusks of a wild boar.
"Charge!" he grunted. "Chaaaaaaarge!"
The terrified dog slunk away.

The grateful hare asked,
"Now, how can I help *you*?"
Cinta had only one request.
"Help me climb that tree
so I can eat all the fruit."

The hare did its best.
"Push *harder*," begged Cinta.
"I am *trying*," gasped the hare.

It was no use.

"I am so very hungry," whimpered Cinta.
"Starving in fact!"

He had a brilliant idea.
On a hilltop he saw the largest castle
he had ever seen. "Perhaps, if I *look* like a king,
the guard will let me in. Perhaps someone will feed me."

"To look like a king, I must have a crown. Today,
I saw three crowns. I will choose what suits me best."
Cinta could picture it easily.

Cinta sighed.
"The truth is,"
he admitted to himself,
"I am not a king.
I am just a hungry pig,
and all alone."

But he was not alone.
A white dove heard him,
and flew off to tell his mate.

Wearily, Cinta wandered down to a river.
He gulped and slurped and then cooled his feet.

A few birds flew by. "I love birds," thought Cinta.
"They fly like angels. I wish I could fly."

Cinta lay back on the riverbank.
He dreamed he flew with angels.

When Cinta awoke, the sun was low in the sky.
More birds flew by. "Are they going home?" he wondered.

"Home!" he exclaimed.
"My pen!
My trough!
My mudbath!"

Cinta bolted over the bridge.
He ran faster than he ever had,
faster than a cheetah by far.
He ran all night long.

To his surprise, Cinta found the gate to his pigpen open.
His master stood there. Cinta expected the worst.
No food.

"Well, Cinta," said his master.
Cinta froze.
His master chuckled. "I must have left the gate unlocked,"
he said, "so you pushed out for a few minutes."
Cinta held his breath.
"I forgot your breakfast," said the master.

Into Cinta's trough, his master poured
six red beets, four yellow carrots
and their green tops,
a purple cabbage, and a round loaf
of brown bread. Cinta gobbled them down.
Then he licked the trough.
Then the bucket.

Cinta rolled into his puddle
and wriggled into the mud.
He crossed his feet
and snuffled with delight.
It was then that he saw his visitors.

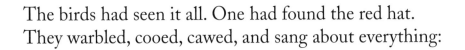

Cinta was thrilled. "My friends!
What a wonderful day!" he exclaimed.
"Sing to me about my great adventure."

The birds had seen it all. One had found the red hat.
They warbled, cooed, cawed, and sang about everything:

      the shepherds and sheep
      the ox, the ass
      the lumpy animals
      the spotted cheetahs
      the three fine kings
      even their monkey
      the hunter and deer
      the hound and the hare
      the castle, the river
      and themselves.

As they sang, Cinta waved his hooves and hat,
keeping time. "I can see it all again!"

The Journey of the Magi fresco travels around three walls of the small Medici Chapel. Above the altar on the fourth wall Cosimo de' Medici placed a painting of Mary and Jesus by Filippo Lippi. The Child is the destination of the kings' long journey. (A copy, made at the time, stands as a substitute for the original panel.)

On either side of the entrance, Benozzo painted shepherds, sheep, the ox and the ass. Inside the alcove, gatherings of angels celebrate the birth of the Child Jesus.

The artist worked in true fresco ('fresh' in Italian), painting onto the walls while the plaster was still damp. He then applied precious lacquers, lapis lazuli and pure gold, that glistened in the candlelight of the chapel.

▶ OPEN AND UNFOLD